Tumpty's plane

Originated by Polly Dunbar

WALKER
ENTERTAINMENT

Tilly and her friends were making paper planes. Tumpty was so excited! He wanted to make his own Tumpty plane!

"I want a bitey, bitey one!"

"Elegant and pretty, just like me!"

"I'm going to fold the paper just like Tilly did,"
said Tumpty.

But it wasn't easy.

"Oh, no ... I can't do it!" he cried.
"I'm too clumsy."

"Don't worry," said Tilly, "we'll help."

So, Hector folded some paper ...

Pru decorated it ...

and Doodle made it bitey, bitey.

Then, Tiptoe added some magic twinkles ...

and the plane was finished!

"Oh! Thanks!" said Tumpty.

"Now we're all ready for

THE GREAT
FLYING
CONTEST!"

said Pru.
And they all
ran off.

But Tumpty wasn't ready...
"I really wanted to make my own Tumpty plane
all by myself," he cried.

Tilly had an idea.

"We're cleared for take-off, Pilot Tumpty."

"Here we go!"

"Look, I made my very own Tumpty plane," said Tumpty.

"Yay, now it really IS time for

THE GREAT
FLYING
CONTEST!"

cheered Hector.

WHOOOOOOSH

The planes flew through the air.

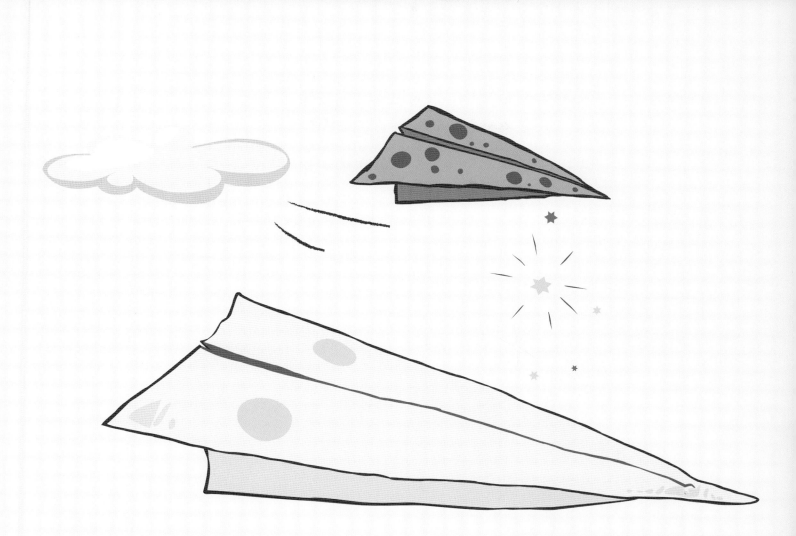

And the winner of
The Great Flying Contest was ...

Tumpty! With the Tumpty Plane!
Everybody cheered.

"Hurray!"

"And," said Tumpty,
"I made it all by myself!"

First published 2014 by Walker Entertainment
An imprint of Walker Books Ltd
87 Vauxhall Walk, London SE11 5HJ

2 4 6 8 10 9 7 5 3 1

© 2012 JAM Media and Walker Productions
Based on the animated series TILLY AND FRIENDS, developed and produced by Walker Productions and JAM Media
from the Walker Books 'Tilly and Friends' by Polly Dunbar. Licensed by Walker Productions Ltd.

This book has been typeset in Gill Sans and Boopee.

Printed in China

British Library Cataloguing in Publication Data:
a catalogue record for this book is available from the British Library

ISBN 978-1-4063-5619-9

www.walker.co.uk

See you again soon!